This is how I Do it with my Lady

Straight to the Point

Lewis Danderidge
7345 Pepper Mill Ln., Memphis, TN 38125
www.Divinealliancepublishing.com

Ordering information: Quantity sales. Special discounts are available on quantity purchases by corporations, associations, and others. For details, contact the "Special Sales Department" at the address above.

Book Cover design by:
Divine Alliance Publishing
Book Layout by:
Divine Alliance Publishing

ISBN 978-0-986161056

Printed in the United States of America

1. Title 2. Author 3. NonFiction

This is how I Do it with my Lady

Straight to the Point

LEWIS DANDERIDGE

Divine Alliance Publishing

Contents

Introduction 1

Chapter 1: My First Time 3

Chapter 2: The Other Lovers 23

Chapter 3: Program Interruption 37

Chapter 4: Paying Off Like Lotto 41

Chapter 5: Fair Exchange 43

Chapter 6: A Bet I Had To Take 45

Chapter 7: The Good Life 61

Chapter 8: Pop-pop 63

Closing Remarks 79

Introduction

I was good to every woman that came into my life, and the ones who met my mother, always told her, "Your son is something else. He sho' know how to make a woman feel like a woman. "Your son isn't anything nice in bed. He will make any woman squirm from head to toe."

My momma's reply would always be, "All of my sons are just like their father: good young men with good hearts. My youngest, though, he's got a big heart, but I'm scared he might break a few in his lifetime. He started charming women the day he was born, and I don't see him stopping any time soon."

Momma wasn't no fool, and her words held true just as grass is green and the sky is blue. I charmed myself into the lives of women who, in return, opened their bodies to me and whatever else they had to offer. I was lucky enough to learn at an early age, that the only thing a woman wants from a man, is to make her feel like a woman. There are different ways to accomplish this, but my choice involved a lot of hard dick, a skillful tongue, and dashes of attentiveness. And just like Colt 45, it worked every time.

Chapter 1

My First Time

I was fifteen when I got my first taste of heaven. It was during Spring Break while I was in the ninth grade. Me and a few of my friends went to the park on a day when it seemed like every girl in the neighborhood was there. I was determined to hook up with at least one and maybe take it to the next level in my journey to becoming a man.

We approached the picnic area like a pack of young wolves, talking jive about who was going to get the number from the finest girl, and who would be stuck with the ugliest one. Before long, we had all gone our separate ways, each of us on the hunt for some action.

I was barely in high school, and that was around the time when older women started catching my eye. It started with Mrs. Golden. She was my sixth grade English teacher, and more times than I could remember, I would catch myself daydreaming about sucking her titties. She was a fine woman with the perfect pair, and many of days I would be sitting at my desk writing down answers while thinking of ways to get close to them titties of hers. I would raise my hand and act like I needed help just so that she could lean over and put them *big thangs* inches from my face while giving me directions on what to do. That's as close as I ever got, but my desire for older ladies started with her. And, as I strolled through the park, my radar went to work, closing in on any woman who looked seasoned to my liking.

After scoping out the entire area, I finally laid eyes on the mocha-colored beauty that seemed ripe for the picking. She was sitting on a bench with another young lady, giggling and smiling when I looked in their direction. Lingering eye contact from a woman is a sure sign that she's interested in some form or fashion, and I was getting it from both of them. I took that as my cue to start my approach.

Cool as a spring breeze, I strutted over with a smile on my face while thinking of some of the slickest shit to say. They were older than me, so I knew my game had to be tight. I could pass for eighteen, but I was hoping my charm and words could make up for any age difference. I locked eyes with my target when I was within a few feet of them.

"How y'all doing, today, ladies?"

She answered for them through juicy, glossed lips. "We're good."

I paused and looked around like I was confused. "I think I'm lost and need some directions."

"Oh, really," she replied, looking concerned and ready to help. "Where are you trying to go?" I checked out my surroundings. "Can you tell me how to get to your heart?"

"Whoa!" Her friend yelled, sliding over and patting the bench. "I think you need to sit down."

"You mind if I sit down?" I asked while not breaking eye-contact.

She was blushing hard, then said, "Boy, how old are you?"

They both seemed interested in my answer, but my game was too tight to be denied.

"Age ain't nothing but a number to tell you how long it's been since you slid out yo' momma's coochie."

Both of them laughed like I was Eddie Richard Pryor or somebody, and that's when I knew I had her. Make a woman laugh, and you'll be in them panties soon after that.

I took the seat in between them as the last of their laughter died down.

Before she knew it, we were looking into each other's eyes. I wanted to reach over and kiss those glossy lips of hers, and she was close enough that I could smell the strawberry scent. I turned my game up another notch.

"Can I ask you a question?"

She smacked her lips. "You never answered mine?"

"Sho' didn't," her girl chimed in, smacking her lips as well. "But say some more of that funny shit and I'll forget about it."

"Well, I only speak the truth, and the truth is, I want to see if I can get to know your friend."

She chuckled, giving me a playful elbow. "Girl, this nigga too smooth. Her name's, Pam, by the way."

"I was getting to that," Pam insisted, reaching across me and pushing her friend's shoulder. Her friend then got up and wondered off, leaving us alone to talk.

I introduced myself and went to work, making her smile more and more with each word. After about ten minutes, I felt like she was digging me, so I popped the big question for any teenager.

"Will you call me if I give you my number?"

She looked away for a second and then rolled her eyes back to me. "Boy how old are you?"

"Old enough to take you out to dinner or a movie."

She was acting like it was a hard decision, but I knew she was with it.

"Yeah, why not."

We talked some more until I saw my friends walking up. I wasn't about to let one of them shoot game at Pam and get it before I did, so I reached into my pocket and gave her a piece of paper.

"That's my number." I glanced over my shoulder to make sure my boys were watching. Call me."

"I will."

I gave her a smile before I got up and jogged over to them. They were checking her out, ignoring me and my puffed-out chest.

"Don't even look that way," I said, waving them off. "That's me right there."

One of them looked back at Pam. "You ain't gon' hit that."

I put my arm on his should and held up a finger. "I'm gon' let you smell it when I do."

Pam called me a couple of days later and we set up a date for the weekend.

I was excited when I told my boys about her calling me and our upcoming date.

"You a virgin and you gon' cum soon as you kiss her," one of them teased, causing all of us to laugh.

Maybe he was right, maybe he was wrong. I was anxious to find out, though.

My money was only long enough for a burger and shake at this spot near Pam's house. We ate and talked, and eventually went to her place to watch some TV afterwards. I knew she was a grown woman when she came out the kitchen with a bottle of wine and two glasses. She sat down and filled both, passing me one with a smile. We sipped, talked and watched TV until the wine took effect, and that's when the conversation turned to sex.

"I'll teach a man how to make love to me," she said, out of the blue.

I didn't know what to say. She kind of scared me, to be honest. "Can I use the bathroom?"

She giggled, pointing with the glass of wine. "It's down that hallway to the right."

I stood up and was afraid that she could see that I was hard. Her words had caused me to rise up like a flagpole, so I turned away as I passed her, hoping she didn't notice. Her giggling continued as I walked down the hall and into the bathroom.

I unzipped my pants and my dick was poking out the hole of my boxers like a snake coming out of its den. It had never been that hard, and for a second, I though it was going to pop like a balloon. I held it down and starting peeing, but it popped back up like a jack-in-the-box and piss splattered all over the toilet and on the floor. I shook my head because I couldn't believe how nervous I was.

I used a lot of toilet paper to clean up the mess, and then washed my hands while looking in the mirror. *You got a fine ass sexy brown frame in there and you scared as hell? You better get yo' ass out this bathroom and go handle that!*

Everything would've been cool if I hadn't been so hard. My johnson was still standing at full attention, throbbing to the point that it was almost hurting. So I whipped it back out and started stroking it, thinking that I could handle myself better if I could cum before going back out there. I quickly gave that up because dry-stroking a hard johnson isn't an enjoyable feeling at all. I just tucked him in my waistband and left out the bathroom, feeling him trying to escape like a caged animal.

I walked pass a bedroom door that was closed when I first went to the bathroom. It was now open, and Pam was sitting on the bed, legs crossed, wineglass in one hand, the other hand rubbing the space next to her. Her jeans and shirt was now replaced with a pink housecoat.

"Come in." Her eyes were glossy and I could tell that the wine was having its way with her.

I took a deep breath and walked slowly to the bed, wearing a smile that was forced and hard to hold. I sat down and I could feel the head of my johnson poke me in my navel.

I guess I wasn't close enough for Pam's liking, because she pulled me closer and took my hand in hers. She then leaned over and kissed me. The smell and taste of the wine was sweet on her tongue when it slid into my mouth.

We kissed for several minutes until she pushed me away and looked me in the eyes while opening her housecoat. Before I knew it, she had placed my hand on her perky brown breast.

"Can you suck on them and rub my pussy while you do it?"

I could feel myself starting to sweat, and I tried to hide how nervous I was. I'm sure I didn't do a good job. And it had to be obvious to her that I didn't know what the hell to do, because she smiled as she grabbed me by the back of my head and slowly pulled me into her awaiting breast. I opened my mouth and got a hard nipple in return. She immediately interrupted me when I started sucking it like a baby during feeding time.

"Do it soft like you're kissing it," she whispered while softly rubbing my head. "Lick it too, baby."

She put me at ease with her directions, and I followed everyone. The more I licked and sucked, the more she squirmed and moaned. I was starting to really get into it because I saw that she was enjoying it. That shit was turning me on.

Pam was moaning and panting when she took my hand and put it in between her legs. I could feel the heat before my fingers touched something that was wetter than water. My fingers began to explore her, sliding up and down while her hips started a motion of their own. It got wetter by the second, and she was on the edge of the bed with her feet on the floor, basically fucking my fingers.

Without warning, she stopped and laid back on the bed, her housecoat opened and showing off her beautiful body.

She was laying there sexy as hell, staring at me, her legs spreading like a peacock's tail. "You ever ate some pussy before?"

I shook my head. "No."

"Well, it's a first time for everything. Come here," She called me with her finger.

I turned around and climbed up on the bed after kicking my shoes off, crawling up between her legs like a bear looking for honey. And that honey was right in front of me, glistening off her soft brown thighs and a clean-shaven mound of something that I had only seen in dirty magazines we found while playing in an old abandoned house.

I stopped when my face was only inches away from her heavenly entrance. She looked down like she was wondering what the holdup was. I gave her a nervous smile and then stuck my tongue out, causing her to giggle.

"Lick it," she replied as she laid back and opened her legs wider.

Hesitant, but eager to give her what she wanted, I aimed my tongue at the wet target and leaned forward. I kept my eyes open because I was observant by nature, and seeing that I was trying to be a frequent visitor to the area, I needed to know how everything worked.

Pam's pussy looked like it was smiling at me sideways, as my hard and steady tongue parted her lips until I was up to my nose in her sweet honey. She tensed up while I went deeper and deeper until I couldn't go any further. Not knowing what the next move was, I did the first thing that came to mind. I shook my head like I was saying "no". After a few shakes, and not getting a big reaction from Pam, I switched it up and nodded my head a few times like I was saying "yes". She squirmed a little, but that was about it. A last-ditch effort was cut short when she asked a question while I was moving my neck like a chicken, going in and out with my tongue.

"Did yo' momma bake cakes sometimes when you were little?"

I stopped just as I was about to go in, wondering if she had a habit of asking out-of-the-blue questions. I didn't know where she was going with it, but I answered with my tongue still hanging out my mouth. "Uh huh."

She was still laying down, her eyes to the ceiling. "So, remember how she used to stir the cake-mix with the eggbeater, and we would be standing there waiting for her to hand us the beaters and the spoon?"

I smiled at the thought. "Yeah, I remember that. Me and my sisters used to fight over who turn it was to get the bowl."

She giggled, her voice soft and sultry. "Okay, so remember how excited you were when you finally got that spoon, and how you licked that spoon until every speck was gone?"

I remembered it like it was yesterday. "I used to lick the hell out of that spoon, too."

"Good." She giggled. "Now I want you to lick my spoon, baby."

Thinking about it that way, caused me to gain a little bit of confidence as I stared at her spoon. The cake mix was waiting for me, so I moved in and split her in half with my tongue, starting from the bottom and licking up until I hit the spot that was obviously the right spot.

"Oh shit!" she, whispered loudly, her body shuttering like she got hit by lightning.

That told me that I was onto something, so I repeated the same motion, starting from the bottom and up to the top until lightning struck again.

"Damn, baby!"

As I was going back down, my eyes stayed glued to the spot. Just to make sure my hunch was right, I slowed my motion and licked that pussy inch by inch while tasting everything she had to offer.

Her hands were on her side, balled into fists that clutched the sheet like she would fall if she let go. That gave me the ego-boost to confidently approach the spot and let my tongue slide across it while watching her for a response. As soon as I reached it, she let out a loud ass yell.

"Fuck!"

Next thing I know, she grabbed my head with both hands and wouldn't let me move from the spot, fucking up my motion and breaking my focus.

"Kiss it right there," she panted, adjusting my head so that my mouth was directly where she wanted it. "Kiss it like you kissed me."

I started kissing girls when I was not even a teenager, so that was something I was good at. This was just my first time trying it with *these* pair of lips. But I wanted to please her, so I puckered up and imagined it was her mouth that I was kissing. Her hips started to roll when I started tonguing the spot, letting the tip swirl around and around while my lips slowly sucked in all of her juices.

"Oooooh shit!"

Her grip on my head got tighter, then she took full control, guiding me all the way to the bottom and back into my original routine. Up to the top, tongue kiss the spot for a second, and then back down. Each time, I could feel her getting wetter. After a few strokes of that, her legs were shaking like a pair of dice.

"Can...can I...come on your tongue?" She was breathing like she just ran from the police.

I was still licking and sucking, but confused at the same time because I didn't know that women could come. I wanted to see this shit, so I nodded my head. "Uh huh."

She looked down at me while releasing my head, her eyes barely open and a slight curl in her lips. Her hands than began to wonder over her body, softly squeezing her breasts before giving each nipple a gentle twist. Apparently, she was getting turned on from touching herself, so I continued watching while thinking about how I was going to touch her the same way.

"I want to cum so bad," she whispered, her fingertips brushing gently down her stomach and stopping right where I had been striking lightning.

In a circular motion, she started massaging the spot with one hand and placed the other one on my head. I could hear the honey stirring inside of her, and it got louder and louder as she continued to rub. Three fingers had her cooking like a Sunday dinner. I observed until she gave me a command.

"Come here." Her fingers kicked into another gear, and she was rubbing that thang like she was trying to start a fire. "Take off you clothes first."

I rolled over off the bed and pulled off my shirt. Pam was still rubbing when she glanced over at me, giggling as she slowed her stroke. I looked down and saw the head of my dick peeking over the waistband. As soon as I unzipped my pants, he sprung out and bounced up and down before coming to a stop. It was pointing straight ahead, right in Pam's direction.

She was staring at it like it was her favorite dessert. "I don't know how old you are, but that thing look full-grown to me."

Maybe I had a growth-spurt or something, because it did look bigger than usual and it was rock-hard like it could break glass. Or, maybe it was because I wasn't locked in the bathroom pulling on my johnson while one of my sisters knocked on the door, breaking my focus from finding the right page in that nasty magazine we found in an abandoned house. Yeah, the woman laying in the bed playing with herself was real, and this was way different than beating my meat.

I stepped out my pants, climbed back into the bed and up right back in between Pam's legs. She raised them up and scooted down a little until my face was right where she wanted it. Her legs then came down on my shoulders, locking me in like I was about to take a ride on a roller coaster. I wrapped my arms around them and prepared for take-off, licking me lips while watching her finger and rub herself.

For some reason I felt more comfortable and ready to do whatever I had to do to please her, and she seemed to notice.

"Okay, I'm ready to come."

She used her fingers to spread herself at the spot where I'd been licking. I was feeling like a contestant on the Price Is Right, waiting as the curtains opened to show me my prize. When it was revealed, Pam gave me instructions while using a finger to point it out to me.

"Lick it right here." She teased it with the tip of her finger, triggering a roll in her hips.

It was pink, and kind of looked like a small nipple. Pam pressed down on it and started rubbing like she was trying to erase it, letting out moans that made my eyes buck.

"Get it, baby!"

She didn't have to tell me twice. My dick was hard and my tongue was even harder, so I let it slide up until it came against the nipple. My first instinct was to latch on to it like a baby at feeding time and suck every ounce of honey out of her. I didn't want to rush it, though. Pam had this laid-back type of vibe to her, so I figured I'd start slow and go from there. I thought about how she used her finger to tease it, and seeing that it got her hips to rolling, I used the tip of my tongue to do the same thing and got the same results.

"Yeah, baby," she purred. "Right there."

I was watching her squirm and grip the sheets but still focused on my job. She was all into in, and that just put me at ease and gave me more and more confidence.

That's when I relaxed and got a little more creative just to see how far I could take her.

I puckered up and added some soft kisses, letting my tongue dance on that nipple between each one. Then, just as I started tongue kissing it real good, Pam grabbed my head with both hands and started shaking like she was going crazy. I felt her legs tighten around my neck and I couldn't move, so I stuck out my tongue and licked whatever I could while she basically fucked my face.

"I'm coming! I'm coming!"

I didn't know where she was going, but I was happy to be right where I was at.

And, as she started guiding my head up and down and getting my face soaked with all of her sweet honey, I thought about how I never imagined pussy could taste so damn good.

Pam's body calmed down after a few shakes and shivers. She gave my head a final rub before her body relaxed and freed me from the hold she had on me. I didn't move, though: my mouth was still a tongue-length away.

Pam exhaled and spoke to the ceiling. "Come on up her and give me some of that thang."

I shook my head. "Not yet."

I guess she was used to me following directions, because she raised up and stared at me, "fuck me" all in her face. But before she could say anything, I leaned all the way in and gave her pussy a soft kiss like I was saying goodbye. I could feel her body go limp as I released and came in again. She was under my spell and now I was in control.

"You gotta' come a few more times and then I'll give you some of this."

Without hesitation, her legs opened wider as she lifted them in the air and pulled them back as far as they could go. I was looking a buffet right in the face, and it was dinner time.

I had Pam coming left and right over the next hour. She was more experienced than I was, but I was a quick learner. She also knew what she liked, so when she told me to put my finger in her ass while I was sucking on her pussy, I wasn't surprised when she came like a waterfall. The more she came, the more I was turned on. By the time I was done, the bed looked like somebody spilled a pot of water on it.

Pam was laying there breathing hard with a hand on her stomach after I had damn near sucked the life out of her. "Baby, if that dick is as good as your tongue, you got some fire shit going on." She got up and climbed out the bed, ass jiggling as she walked to the door. A sexy grin was on her lips when she glanced over her shoulder. "I might not ever let you leave."

She let out a sinister laugh that echoed off the walls as she disappeared down the hall. Little did she know, that's exactly what I wanted to hear.

The big wet spot in the center of the bed was proof that I was holding my own as a first-time tongue-slanger. It was a proud moment for me. I sat there admiring the work

I put in until Pam came back in the room with two glasses of water. She handed me one and stood in front of me while she took a drink from hers.

"You sure that was your first time eating coochie?" Her hand went to her hip after taking a sip.

I tried to hide my smile by taking a drink of the cold water. The girl had me blushing and shit. I downed the whole glass and licked my lips. "Yeah, first time."

She studied me as she took another sip before taking my glass and placed them on the nightstand. My legs opened when she came close enough, and I was met with a stiff-arm to the chest. I fell straight back on the bed and my dick was pointing straight up in the air. Next thing I know, I felt Pam grab it with both hands.

I reached for a pillow and propped it behind me so that I could have a good view.

"Damn it's big and pretty." She was holding it like a baseball player checking for a good bat, all while biting her bottom lip. "I wonder how it taste."

Before I could say anything, she started licking on that mofo like a melting ice cream cone. Her tongue went up to the top, licked the tip and made its way back down.

A tilt of the head allowed her to give the other side the same treatment without missing a beat. I had to stop my leg from shaking when she reached the top again and let her lips wrapped around the head. The fit was perfect. And then, right before my eyes, she went down and made half of it disappear. Shit was magical.

I think I was a little too big for her to take it all, but I appreciated the attempt. I also appreciated how warm that mouth was, and how sexy her lips looked while she held her pose and gave me a wink with a mouth full of dick. At that point, I realized that Pam had probably done this at least once or twice before.

She came to her knees and put one hand on my stomach. I closed my eyes and laid back as her other hand started stroking me nice and slow, causing my dick to jump in her mouth. That seemed to hit a switch, because I could feel Pam sucking like a vacuum cleaner as her head rose to the top. She held my dick at an angle so that it pressed against her tongue, and my toes balled into fist from the sensation. I wanted to tell her I loved her when she gave my head a last hard suck when she pulled it from her mouth.

I opened my eyes and peeked down at her. She was holding my dick like she was about to make an announcement.

"You like that?"

From the devilish smile she gave me, she knew damn well I liked it. I just nodded my head and smiled.

She was still stroking it. "What else do you like?"

"Shit, whatever you do, I guess." I hunched my shoulders.

"Well," she said as she pushed my pole back and lowered her head. "Do you like this?"

I ended up answering that question a few times while Pam licked, sucked and kissed wherever she could, and the answer was either "yeah" or "hell yeah". The fact that she was thoughtful enough to ask, was something that I really liked about her. It let me know that she was taking a liking to me, and this wasn't no one-way street. I mean, from the way she was sucking my dick, I damn near felt like she loved me. She was slurping and stroking and looking like she was enjoying it the whole time. If she was aiming to please, she was damn sure accomplishing her mission. I wasn't about to be outdone, though. She had me stiff and hard like a flagpole, and I was planning on making her salute this mofo by the time I was done.

Pam got her last taste and pulled it out her mouth with a plop. It was wet with a shine to it, and she was holding it and staring at it like it was the prettiest dick in the world.

"Can I have some now?"

Her tone was soft, like a kid asking for some candy. She wasn't asking, though.

I was forced to roll over when she laid on side of me without letting go of what she obviously wanted bad as hell. When I was in between her legs, I pushed up and watched her play with her new toy. She was sliding the head up and down on her pussy and then

started slapping it against her like a drumstick, gasping and squirming while she looked me dead in the eyes the whole time.

I could feel the heat and hear the splash. I just didn't know what to do next after she held it still and put the tip in. She closed her eyes and put her warm hands on my waist, and I guess she was leaving the rest up to me; a virgin. So, I did what any virgin would do: I fell on top of her and started hunching like a dog.

"Ouch, boy!" Pam squealed, her two hands pushing me in the stomach before I could go all in. I stopped like we were playing freeze-tag, hoping I didn't hurt her. Her facial expression told me that I better not try that shit again.

"Who be letting you fuck them like that?" She glanced up at me and then looked back down. Seeing half of my dick in her changed her attitude real quick. Her voice voice turned sweet as pie. "You can't be just ramming that big ole thing in nobody."

"I'm sorry." I didn't know what else to say, mainly because I was too in tuned with how wet and warm she was.

Pam wiggled around up under me and seemed to be back comfortable. Her hands went back to my waist. An encouraging smile. "Kiss me."

I lowered my head real slow while making sure I didn't hurt her again. Half in already, I was able to stay on my knees as we kissed. Once our tongues touch, her hips started rolling while I stayed still until further noticed.

She whispered in between kisses. "You have to be gentle first."

It was like she was dancing on my dick the way she was swaying them hips.

"This pussy ain't going nowhere." Her eyes rolled in back of her head for instant, and then met mine. "Just work your way in. You don't have to kick in the door."

We both laughed but she didn't miss a stroke. She kept on until she needed more.

"Give me that dick, baby."

I wasn't about to fuck it up again. The only way to go was to spoon-feed her a little at a time, so gave it to her inch-by-inch as she opened her legs wider and wider.

"Yes, baby," she cooed, her tempo slowing down until she was still.

Her lips reached for mine as I slid in further. The deeper I went, the harder she kissed me. That led to her sucking on my tongue when I had gone as far as I could go.

She was breathing real heavy as we kissed. Our bodies went still, and that's when I realized how hot she actually was. My dick felt like it was in a sauna.

"Mmmm, you feel good." She gave me an intense stare. "Now be gentle."

It started as amateur hour for me, but I closed the show out like a world-class porn star. I give Pam most of the credit, though. She let me know what she liked and I just followed instructions.

Even while she was riding me or taking every inch while I hit it from the back, she gave me game on how to work with what I was working with. She claimed that I was about average, and that sex was about feeling good and not about trying to beat the pussy up unless it's requested. She made me aware of that out the gate, so for the rest of the night, I made sure that she got this dick the right way.

That night was the first of many nights we spent together. It lasted for a couple of years, and for the most part, all we did was fuck. Going at it three or four times a day became normal for us. It was almost like we were addicted to one another. I would be playing basketball with my boys, and Pam would cross my mind. My dick would get hard on the spot and I'd walk right off the court and be at her house shortly after. And there were even times when we would go two or three days without leaving the bedroom unless it was for food. Yeah, we had a lot of sex.

All that fucking didn't come without the obvious eventually happening. Pam got pregnant a year into our relationship, something I wasn't thinking about while I was constantly coming inside her with no regard. She had a miscarriage early on, though, so we had no other bond between us except for the sexual chemistry that we had shared for a few years. After a while, we started seeing other people, which eventually led us to go our separate ways. I took with me the ability to please a woman, and Pam left having had experienced the best sex of her life. Even to this day when we cross paths, she'll smile and tell me that I'm still the best she ever had.

Chapter 2

The Other Lovers

High school was where I polished my game on girls my age just so it was tight for the older ladies after I got out of school. Don't get me wrong, I wouldn't pass up a girl my age if I was digging her. They just didn't have enough experience for me.

My tongue and dick game was just a little too strong for them. A lot of guys my age thought a clitoris was a dinosaur, so the young chicks didn't stand a chance with me. I knew their pussy better than they did, and turning them out would've only led to a lot of unnecessary drama for me. I didn't have time for busted windows or being stalked by some chick who wanted to keep me all to themself. What I had was so good that I didn't think it was fair to just share it with one woman. And, as you'll see, sharing has always been one of my best qualities.

But, there *was* this one young lady that caught my eye to the point that I decided to make an exception and put something on her that she wouldn't ever forget.

By the time I was a senior, my mind was made up about the kind of life I wanted for myself. I needed to be in the company of fine women at all times, and money was the key to that life. Wherever there's a nigga with money, pussy ain't too far behind.

I learned that early. I was working a job that paid decent for a kid my age, but my mentality was just on some grown man shit. And to live like a grown man, my money had to be just as long as my dick. With the job as my only source of income, I was coming up short as hell, though. That problem was solved when I decided to supplement my income by getting into the dope game. Once that happened, the life I wanted to live began to materialize right before my eyes. That life included a lot of sex, and I welcomed it with an open zipper.

The city was having a dance that brought all of the high schools together for one big night. Of course, I was dressed to impress and had on some panty-dropping cologne for the ladies. I also had fifty copies of my phone number with me because I always played with the odds. The more I gave out, the better chances I had to hit the vagina jackpot, and I passed them out like party fliers. I was stepping to all the finest women in the place, too. Unfortunately, I left with twenty still in my pocket. I didn't really think I would pass out that many for real, but I was confident that something good would come from my hard work. Eventually, it did.

I got about fifteen callbacks out of the thirty numbers I passed out, but only about ten of them really kept my attention. Different women bring different things to the table, and this one pretty mofo was an entree and dessert that I just couldn't pass up.

Her name was "Brina". Out of all the women I met at the dance, she was the one I clearly remembered when she first called me. I was crazy about women with that creamy caramel complexion, so she was stuck in my head from the time I saw her. I only kicked game with her for a few minutes while I was there. We laid eyes on each other when I first came in the door. She was with her friends and I wanted to check out the rest of the scene. When I slid her my number, she said something slick and gave me a smile.

It made me want to lift her dress and eat that pussy right then and there. Women with slick mouths and snotty attitudes have the best head, at least from my experiences. They suck a dick like they got something to prove, and for the most part, they've always made me a believer. From the look in her eyes, I knew she had some fire.

We talked on the phone for two weeks before we met in person again. By then, we knew a lot about each other and there was most definitely some chemistry between us.

She sho' could talk shit, too. Mofo made a brother laugh and get hard at the same damn time. I couldn't wait to see her.

The night of our date, I picked her up and was drunk off her as soon as she got in my car. She was wearing a brown skirt with a black top that hugged some nice-sized titties, and she was smelling good as hell. Her hair was cut like she was down with Salt-n-Pepa. I looked at her thick ass thighs as she put on her seat belt, and could see that she was a four-course meal and then some.

She sucked her teeth with a smile. "You staring at me like you want to eat me or something."

"Shit," I replied, licking my lips. "You must be kin to Ms. Cleo, because you reading my motha-fuckin' mind."

She slapped my arm. "Drive, nigga."

We decided to go to the movies after riding around for a minute. It gave me a chance to set the tone for the rest of the night. I had my arm around her the whole time, whispering in her between the action while she ate popcorn from the bucket we were sharing.

"Girl, do you taste as good as you smell?"

"I know this popcorn good, though." She reached in the bucket and tossed some in her mouth.

I liked her game, I'll admit. Mine was still too strong. I let my tongue brush against her ear as I whispered. "I just want to romance that clit and see how many times you can cum on my tongue."

I could feel her body shake when I licked her ear again. Her eyes were closed like she was coming. She took a second before she responded.

"Don't do that no more." She smacked her lips and looked at the screen. "You gone get yo'self in some shit you can't handle."

"Well, after I handle it, you gon' need an ice-pack and a motrin for that pussy."

She tried hold her in her laugh but couldn't.

We went back to my place after the movie. I was rubbing her leg on the ride over, and even tried to get a feel of that cat before she slapped my wrist. She was cool until I tried to pull them panties to the side. I knew she was ready, though. That was clear as soon as we stepped in the door.

I didn't even get the chance to hit the lock before she had her tongue down my throat. The sexual tension had built up since I first picked her up, and we both went at each other like two wild animals. Our hands were rubbing and feeling as I guided her over to the couch, bumping into the cocktail able without breaking our kiss. I had a handful of pussy and used one finger to slide in her. She was wetter than a swimming pool and I was ready to backstroke in that mofo.

I raised her blouse and with one hand and kissed on her stomach while I used my other hand to unsnap her bra. I was an expert at unsnapping bras with one hand, and my tongue was at the ready when them beautiful brown titties were released. I lifted her bra and admired nipples that stood up like Hersey kisses. I licked and sucked on them until she put her hands on my shoulders. I knew exactly what she wanted, so I made my way down to her stomach, kissing her belly button while I lifted her skirt and pulled them panties down. I could smell that unmistakable scent of marinating pussy being released as they touched her ankles. It was dinner time.

She kicked her panties to the side when I went to go lick her thigh. I was squeezing her ass and pulling her to me as she opened her legs wide enough to let my tongue slide up in her. The taste made me feel like Popeye when he popped that can of spinach.

Her knees damn-near went limp when I sucked on her while I let my tongue massage her love tunnel. I had to hold her up before she fell on me.

A had big smile on my face. "Shit got you drunk, huh?"

She tried to play it cool as she kicked her flats off. "Nigga, I just lost my balance because of these shoes."

"Well, lose yo' balance again and lay yo' ass back right there," I said, gesturing down at the couch.

Her nose was turned up as she rolled her eyes. She looked around the room for the first time, nodding her head while checking out the furnishings. My couch must have gotten her approval, as well.

She looked at it before sitting down, the attitude that turned me on, still intact.

"I don't know what you want me to lay back for." She got up on all fours, ass in the air, her pumpkin pie peeking at me as she slowly crawled to the end of the couch.

She took one of the big throw pillows and put it behind her as she lay back against the arm. "You ain't gone do shit."

Her legs were cocked wide open. We didn't waste time to take any clothes off except for her panties, so her skirt was still pulled up around her waist. She adjusted her bra-strap by putting her hand under her blouse and pulling it back up on her shoulder but left it unsnapped. As strange as it was, seeing her partially dressed seemed like some freaky shit. And, me being the freak I was, that shit was right up my alley.

I was about to go right in and take care of my business, just to show this little girl exactly who she was dealing with. That mouth had me psyched-up. She was about to eat her words and some dick.

My first instinct was to just dive in and take over her body and shut her up quick as hell. But I wanted to get in her head-first, fuck with her mind and basically own her even when she wasn't in my presence.

I kept a neutral face and said, "Rub it for me."

"What?" Her head tilted like I was speaking Spanish.

"Rub it for me." I nodded my head downward. It took her a second to catch on.

"Boy, I don't play with myself."

She said it like I asked her to eat a pile of dog shit. I could tell that she took her clit for granted, and all she needed was a nigga like to show her why she should thank the good Lord every day for blessing her with such a glorious piece of anatomy.

Don't you want to please me like I want to please you." I made it sound sincere.

Women love sincerity. I could see the wheels turning in her head.

"Yeah." She moved some hair from her face. "But I ain't about to play with myself. If I do that, what I need you for?

I unzipped my pants and whipped out on her. "Because after you rub it, you can play with this."

It was already hard but looked a little ashy. I spit in my hand and started stroking it right there while she watched. She couldn't take her eyes of it. The more I stroked, the more she seemed to be going into some kind of trance. She was dick-matized.

"Take that shit off."

Her blouse went to the floor along with her bra. The skirt was still around her waist, but seeing that I wasn't in the way of anything, I left it alone.

"Rub it for me." I took a couple of steps and stood over her, pipe-hard. Her eyes didn't move but her hand slowly moved from her side and stopped on her leg. When I did the spit thing the first time, I noticed how she squirmed in her seat; nothing got by me, so, of course I was going to try it again.

As soon as I spit in my hand, her eyes shot up right to mine. I paused with my hand to my mouth. She was staring at me like a cat, waiting for my next move. Her hand was near her thigh.

I lowered my hand in slow-motion and wasn't surprised when her eyes followed it every step of the way. I palmed the head and rubbed it in like lotion, one hand on my waist, feeling like I had full control.

"Rub that pussy for me, baby." My stroke was long and slow.

I sensed hesitation, so I quickly brought my hand to my mouth, bringing her eyes right along with me. Before I spit again, I said, "Girl, rub that pussy."

I spit and watched her hand inch closer and closer. Once I got the stroke to going,

I got on some whispering shit.

"If you can't make yo'self feel good, nobody can." Slow-stroking. "Get it wet for me and you can have as much of this as you can take."

Finally, her hand was covering the cute little bush she had, but I didn't see no fingers moving. No problem at all.

After hitting a couple more strokes, I sat down and moved in between her legs. It was funny that her usually smart-mouthed ass hadn't said a word. I wanted to laugh in her face, but instead, I lowered my head and spit on her pussy. No soon as she realized what I had done, her hand went right where the spit was.

"That's right," I said, coaching like Phil Jackson, "Rub it in good, baby."

She was staring at me like she couldn't believe what she was doing, but that didn't stop her. Three fingers were rubbing the lips and she was scooting up on the arm of the couch, trying to get away from her own hand. If I hadn't grabbed her leg, she would've fell off the couch and crashed right on her back. Both of my hands were on her thighs, so to calm her down a little bit, I started massaging and talking to her.

"You like how that feels?" I cupped her chin and kissed her.

She nodded, breathing heavy without saying a word. I keep a straight face and put my arms up under her legs and pulled her to me. The hair between her legs brushed up against my stomach when I lifted her up, and I could also feel how wet she was. She

gave no resistance while I positioned her so that she was laying down with her upper-body was propped-up by the pillow. I wanted to make sure she had a good view.

"Okay." I said, laying on the couch and getting in between her legs, my face inches away from her pussy. "Let me show you where the real party at."

She had a finger in her mouth, looking down at me while I parted her until I saw her clit show its pretty little face. And pretty it was. It looked like a rose that was ready to bud. I got right over it and let a line of spit dribble from my mouth. It watered her rose perfectly. I saw her hand coming from out the corner of my eye. But, before she could reach it, my fast reflexes allowed me to grab her by the wrist. I had to strain because she was hellbent on getting to it.

"Hold on, baby." I looked at her, but she was focused on one thing. "Let me see your hand."

Slowly, I could feel her relax. I then turned her hand palm up and put the index and middle fingers together.

"Use these two," I instructed like a caring teacher. "You'll thank me later."

She looked at her fingers and gave me a glance. I shot her a reassuring smile.

My word was everything to me, and I saw in her eyes that she trusted every word I spoke.

"Okay." I let go of her wrist. "Rub it for me."

I thought she was going to go straight at it, but that wasn't the case at all. Her approach was that of a cautious explorer discovering new territory. Index and middle looked like a weapon in rock, paper, scissors. The closer she got, the more excited I got.

For me, it was a slow tease that I knew was be worth the wait. I shot her a last second instruction.

"Keep 'em together, baby."

From the way she listened, I understood why she stayed on the honor roll. Them fingers adjusted right before contact and hit the target perfectly. Brina sucked it air and flinched but her fingers never moved. She went still as if she was getting used to the feel of everything.

"Try going in a slow circle first and see how you like it."

No hesitation at all. She was soft and gentle with it. Her eyes got bigger after a few seconds.

"How does it feel?" I puckered my lips and blew some air while she got that circular motion down to a science.

She could barely talk through the gasps she was releasing. "G... go...good." Her fingers lifted up. "Spi...spit on it again."

That was a request I accommodated with the quickness. I couldn't resist slapping my tongue on that pussy one time before doing it, though. Girl tasted like straight candy and I had a sweet tooth that was hard to satisfy. It filled my mouth with enough moisture to give her everything she wanted, so I let it roll off my tongue. Bullseye.

Surprisingly, her fingers didn't move an inch. I was actually shocked. When my eyes met her I was greeted with a hard stare.

She sucked her teeth while rolling her eyes. "Spit on it, nigga!"

"Oh, you back?" I gave her a cool chuckle, and then hauled off and spit on her pussy like she was a Civil Rights protester in a KKK meeting.

She shook her head and smacked those damn lips before calmly turning her attention back to her new soaked friend. I checked her fingers and her form was cool for a beginner. When they hit that wetness, the sound was music to my ears.

The circular motion didn't start until she let her fingers play in the wetness like a kid splashing in a puddle. It seemed to get her more aroused because her nipples grew even bigger with ever little tap. I was tempted to let my tongue join her in the fun, but I chilled and talked her through the process.

"You see how good that feels?"

"Ye..yeah."

After a couple minutes of getting to know herself, she started using one finger and picked up her pace. Pretty soon, she was hitting that mofo like a DJ scratching a record.

I could feel a vibration come through her body, and I knew she was near the point of exploding. It took everything in me to hold myself back from sucking her pussy while she was coming.

"Are you about to make yourself cum?" I knew the answer, but I asked just so she would realize what was about to happen.

"I..I am."

"Well, cum for me, baby."

I stroked her thighs while she went into a shaking fit. Them beautiful titties of hers were jiggling as she continued to rub one out. She was heaving and sucking in air the entire time, and I realized that it ain't nothing as sexy as seeing a woman cum.

Her shakes lasted for a minute or so. An exhausted but pleasant look on her face was that of a marathon runner who just crossed the finish line. I felt a sense of pride in knowing that I played a small part in her victory.

"So, what you think?"

She put her hands over her face, giggling and shit. "Why you make me do that?"

"I asked you."

That response got a knee to my side.

"I know you liked that shit."

"You don't know a damn thing." She gave me another knee.

"I bet you play with it again."

A pause came with a bashful smile. "So."

I put both of my hands under her butt and lifted her so that her pussy was close enough to kiss. "Well, all I want you to know is…" I took her lips into mine and sucked on them real slow before letting them slide out my mouth. "Them fingers of yours ain't got shit on me."

My penmanship was never that good in school, but I proceeded to use my tongue to write my name in perfect cursive all over Brina's pussy. Every "I" was dotted and every "T" was crossed when I was done with her. She came three more times, and I allowed her to explode in my mouth every rip. I didn't let her take a break because she just kept grinding on my face like she was glued to it after coming like a broken dam. I thought she was done after the third time, but I guess she had one more in her. And, obviously, she saved the best for last.

I was tracing my initials on her clit and sucking it masterfully when I heard those magic words.

"I'm coming again!"

That's when I slid my tongue deep in her love tunnel and waited for the big wave like a kid at the water park. Her legs were shaking, and I could tell that she was about to let loose. But what made the scene even more beautiful, is when I saw her fingers make their way right above my nose and onto her throbbing clit. She started massaging that mofo and I followed her rhythm with my tongue. We were on the same beat. And, as she came all in my mouth, I watched feeling like I had made a great contribution in her life. She had discovered the liberating feeling of self-satisfaction, orgasms-on-demand.

And, in the future, whenever she played with her pussy, no matter where she's at in the world, she'll always know that I was responsible for introducing her to that very pleasure.

So, let the choir say, "Amen."

Chapter 3

Program Interruption

I went into my twenties living real good for a guy my age. No matter how good the money was from the dope game, I always kept a job. The streets were unpredictable, so it was also good to have some for-sure money coming in every week. It also gave me something to do every day. I never was the type to just sit around. If I wasn't at work, I was chasing money and women, and at the same damn time.

All while I was doing my thing, I thought I was the slickest nigga in the world.

Having a job while in the game seemed to give me an advantage and offer me some sort of camouflage to move freely through the streets. But I soon found out that the feds don't give a fuck about none of that shit.

I got caught up on a cocaine case and ended up doing three years in federal prison. Luckily, for me, my case happened a few years before the whole "War Against Drugs" campaign and the mandatory-minimums that were put into law in the late-80's. I got a slap on the wrist compared to what I would've gotten under those laws. But, for a mofo like me, it was the longest three years of my entire fucking life.

Federal prison wasn't bad at all for prison, I guess. They had shit to keep you busy, but I was used to occupying my time in the presence of a woman. Being around a bunch of niggas twenty-four seven, just wasn't for me. Not being able to feel the soft skin of a woman for years at a time, was inhumane treatment in itself. That was enough of a punishment for me. And, after jacking my dick in shower stalls while visualizing some of the best scenes of my sexual past for three years, I promised myself that I wasn't doing anything else to jeopardize my freedom.

Being away from women for so long, helped me to gain a new-found appreciation for everything about them. It didn't go quite beyond the physical, but it was appreciation, nonetheless. So, never again was I going to take for granted a woman allowing me into her body. When I'm offered some pussy, I take it as one of the highest honors a man could possibly have. Ain't nothing like the touch of a woman. A man could be having a bad day, but put a little pussy in his life, and all is well. It could rain for forty days and forty nights, but if he getting his dick sucked, every day is filled with sunshine. They say money rules the world, but in a man's world, pussy is king. We only chase money so that we can have access to the real prize.

Pleasing was my thing, but when I came home from prison, I felt like I had to take it up a notch. Seeing that I wasn't selling drugs anymore, having a job was my only source of income, which was something I wasn't accustomed to. I still had a taste for the finer things in life, so I to come up with a way to satisfy my appetite without finding my ass back in prison.

I had a brother who was a pimp up in D.C. He had money up the ass and a stable full of fine women. It was him who put the thought in my head to get into pimping, seeing that a smooth talk game was something that ran in the family. I had the smoothest by far, and everybody knew that. I could talk a nun into selling some pussy to a priest on a Sunday, and with little effort. It seemed to be the perfect occupation for me to jump into. But, after careful consideration, I decided it just wasn't for me. The money was the aim, but I wanted the pussy, too.

Because I held sex in such high regard, and thought it was the greatest discovering in the history of mankind, it just didn't seem fair to have women out there fucking men as their job. I didn't know too many people who actually loved their job, and I didn't think that turning tricks was any different than going to work in a hot ass plant every day. And, regardless if a woman loved sex like I did, it just wasn't enjoyable with any and everybody. She wasn't going to cum if some trick had her bent over in a dark alley rushing to get his nut off. Sex is one of the greatest pleasures of life, and to subject a woman to sex without orgasms, just didn't sit well with me. And seeing that I had to sample what I was going to be putting out on the streets, I was pretty sure it was going to be pure hell for them girls to fuck some little dick white boy for a couple of minutes after I put this dick and tongue on them. I didn't want to put them through that.

So, I found other ways to supplement my income while doing what I loved to do, and it all came quite naturally.

Chapter 4

Paying Off Like Lotto

When I came home from prison and started catching up with some of the women I messed with before I went in, every last one of them were happy about finally getting some good sex. It was like they had been in the desert and I was a big pitcher of ice water that had finally arrived to quench their thirst. Apparently, two-minute brothers had become the trend, and guys were busting a nut and getting right up before the woman could even get wet. Shit was disrespectful if you asked me. But I was home and ready to bone.

Being the hustler that I was, I saw opportunity in what I was hearing. I had something that was in high demand, something that women wanted but was hard to find.

It was a drought on good dick, and I was walking around with the ability to make a woman's pussy rain for forty days and forty nights. That had to be worth something, especially when every clit in sight had been neglected since I'd been gone. I wasn't about to outright sell dick like some male prostitute standing on a corner or nothing like that. I was just going to let it be known that my time was valuable, and orgasms didn't come for free.

Chapter 5

Fair Exchange

My preference for older women, fell right in line with my plans. Unlike young chicks, they could handle me in the bedroom, and I never had to worry about looking in my rearview and seeing one of them tailing me. Their experience was another thing I appreciated about them, which meant I could pull out every trick in my sexual bag and be allowed to leave without questions about where I was going or when I was coming back.

As long as an older woman got her some good dick on the regular, life was grand. She could focus on shit like bingo and baking cookies with their grandkids instead of worrying about me. Yeah, and when I say I dated "older" women, I don't mean five or ten years older. That was too young for a mofo like me. Twenty-five years older was about the average age-difference. I never went under twenty, though. And, like I said, it paid off big time. Literally.

You see, the older women I dealt with were established in their careers, and in some cases, retired. Having been through a lot of bad marriages and relationships, life as an older, single black woman seemed to be about enjoying grandkids, traveling, playing bingo and getting some good dick in between. Most of them seemed to have given up on growing old with somebody and spending their last days with the person they loved.

And, unfortunately, it was mainly because of guys like me who just couldn't seem to keep our dick in our pants around other women. So, seeing that a fairytale ending just wasn't in the cards for them, they settled for the happy endings that I provided whenever I got hold of that pussy.

Women, by nature, are loving, caring, and will go above and beyond for a man they love, or who makes them feel loved while their fucking them. That's what I did when a woman gave me her body. Even if I didn't love her, her body would think otherwise while I was doing my thing. And when this happened, she would go all out for me, even though I wasn't her man. I can't say that I took advantage of women, but I did use it to my advantage sometimes.

There were other times when women wanted me so bad, that they would do whatever they could to get me, just like when a man sees a woman that he wants. There was nothing different when it came to my situation. It was just sort of a role reversal where I was benefiting financially.

Chapter 6

A Bet I Had To Take

Working as a butcher in a grocery store, was where I met a lot of women. I was twenty-eight at the time, and it was a usual thing for me to flirt with women while I was getting them whatever they wanted. I would throw complements at them like roses, and they would always leave with a smile on their face after I served them the meat of their choice. It was also the place where I met a woman who had to put here money where her mouth was after I licked a brand-new Corvette our that pussy.

She was a forty-nine-year old pretty mofo who was a regular customer at the store. When we first saw each other, I knew I was going to be in between them legs eventually. Brown-skinned and curvy as a mountain road, she fit the description for my prescription, and I needed a heavy dose of her. The thing was, she was playing hard to get. I played right along with her, though, knowing that the look in her eyes was one of pure lust.

"You're a handsome young man."

It was the first thing she ever said to me. Her business-like attire told me that she had a good job, and she had this thing about her that I would call confidence. It was in her graceful walk, and the eye-contact she gave me when I looked up.

I gave her a smile. "Thank you, and I'm sure you get tired of men telling you how fine you are, so I'll just say that "fine" or "beautiful" can't do you any justice."

The compliment didn't seem to phase her. Her attention went to the fresh meat and seafood stored below in the cooler that separated us. She tapped on the glass. "May I have two pounds of the ground sirloin and a pound of the jumbo shrimp?"

I slid open the door to the cooler and started putting her order together. The shrimp were the first thing I grabbed. She kept her eyes on me while I weighed out her pound.

"My daughter's your age." She had a smirky smile on her face, teasing me. "I think you might like her."

I politely denied her suggestion, smiling while shaking my head. "Nawl, she's too young for me. Thanks, though."

"Once you see her, I think you might change your mind."

She said it confidently and with the pride only a mother could have. I played along while putting her shrimp in a bag.

"Does she look like you?"

Blushing. "People say she does. And she's smart."

I nodded and took the sirloin out the cooler. "Is she as sexy as her mother?"

"Boy, don't flirt with me." She looked around with her hand covering her mouth to hide a smile that couldn't be hid. "I'm old enough to be your mother."

"Well, I know I didn't come out your pussy, but I'm damn sure trying to get up in it."

When she rolled her eyes and laughed, I knew I had her. Women love dirty talk when it comes at the right time. And from the way she was blushing and carrying on, I knew that my timing was perfect.

"Give me my meat so I can get out of here," she giggled while waving me off.

I reached over the counter and handed her the packages, staring her right in the eyes. "I'm trying to give you all the meat you can handle."

She playfully snatched the meat and smack her lips. "I'm bringing my daughter with me next time."

"Bring her." I shrugged my shoulders. "I just want you to come."

She shook her head and walked off.

"As many times as you want."

I could hear her laugh as she turned down the dairy aisle.

About a month went by with us flirting with each other and just talking shit. The sexual tension had built up on my end, and I was sure that she was feeling the same way.

Whenever I saw her pushing a grocery cart in my direction, my dick would jump out of my boxers and I would lick my lips and imagine I was tasting her juices. She really had me going, and we hadn't even touched each other yet. Ain't nothing like getting to know someone before having sex. I didn't do that shit often, but I enjoyed the rare occasion when it did happen. We had shared parts of our lives, and I knew it was only a matter of time before we were going to be sharing all of our bodies.

I was on the customer side of the counter restocking seafood batter when I heard the click-clacking of a pair of heels coming my way. Her perfume tickled my nose before her cart came to a stop on side of me. She smelled delicious as always. I shot her a smile while putting the last bag of batter in its place.

"You didn't bring your daughter with you today?"

She blew air between a pretty set of lips that seemed to have been recently touched up with a lip gloss of sort.

"I will one day." She stepped away from the cart and began looking down at the cooler, inching closer and closer to me. "Just don't say I didn't tell you so when you fall in love with her and leave your wife."

Yeah, I told her about me being a married man. It seemed to be the butt of every joke since she found out, always throwing it in my face and laughing about it. She respected my honesty, though. After being lied to so much, most women seemed to welcome honesty, and that's the only thing they were getting from me, straight-up, no chaser. I didn't mind giving a woman the power to decide if she would fuck with me or not, based on my being married. Of course, I shouldn't have gotten married if I wasn't ready to be faithful. But hey, I ain't never said I was perfect.

We had never been as close as we were at that moment. It was actually the first time that I wasn't behind the counter when she came in the store. I took that as a sign to shoot my shot, and I never missed a layup.

"Your daughter or my wife ain't got nothing to do with this."

When she turned around, our faces were inches apart.

"Oh, is that so?" She asked in a whisper.

I nodded, cool as ice, licking my lips so that the words came out smoothly. I was staring into her soul. "Yeah, this is about us, about me and you learning each other's body, enjoying the moment, you know? Let's be friends."

She hadn't moved an inch. I could see a relaxed look come to her face, like my words were massaging her soul. That's when I reached in and kissed her, making sure I gave her bottom lip a little suck before she pulled back. It only lasted a few seconds, but I felt the sparks that had been brewing between us.

"Boy," she whispered while frantically casing the area. "I can't be caught in public kissing a married man."

"Well, let me take you out and we can try this in private."

She laughed as she looked around. "Do it again."

"What?"

"Kiss me."

I gave her what she wanted. It went a little longer than the first time, and I was under the impression that she hadn't been kissed in a while. From the way she eased her tongue in my mouth, I knew damn well that she didn't give a fuck about me being married. Shit, I guess I didn't either, because my tongue was tangled up right along with hers.

I was the one who pulled back after realizing she wasn't about to end the kiss anytime soon. She was a good kisser and I couldn't wait to taste those lips again. I put the pressure on her while she seemed to still be focused on my lips.

"So, this means I can take you out, right?"

"Boy, didn't I say you're too young for me?" She got behind her cart and guided it by me and down toward the dairy section, glancing back at me as she added more sway in her hips.

The next time I saw her, I did manage to get her phone number. It was obvious that she liked to be chased like most women do, which I didn't mind at all. The chase was always my favorite part, especially since I always caught my prey. And from the way she carried herself, I knew she was worth the chase.

My persistence finally paid off when she agreed to let me take her out on a date after talking on the phone several times. I kept her laughing and showed her all the attention I could while being a married man. The subject never came up while we talked, though, and I figured she just was a woman who wanted what she wanted. Eventually, I found out exactly what she wanted.

We were strolling on the riverfront after dinner at a restaurant she was very familiar with. It was a nice spot in the middle of downtown, where waitresses called her by name and the manager came out to speak while we were eating. She seemed to garner respect that was reserved for people who had money to spread around wherever they went. I liked her style, too, especially when she pushed my money to the side after I tried to pay the bill. She wouldn't even let me tip, and that's when I knew she was worth the chase.

I never asked what she did for a living, and she never mentioned it when we talked. Her attire was always business-like and very classy, so I assumed she was a professional of some sort. It didn't really matter to me. My pockets weren't like they used to be, but I was content with being in the company of somebody who had it like that.

You see, when you're around money, chances are, it'll rub off on you one way or another. I wasn't the sharpest knife in the drawer, but I knew everything about money.

We came to a bench on the walkway and took a seat facing the river while darkness set over downtown Memphis. Being that it was a weeknight, the riverfront was practically empty except for a group of white teenagers huddled around with skateboards in their hands. We watched them pass a joint around in circles, each one adjusting their long hair before they took a hit. Once the last hit was taken, their wheels hit the concrete and rolled off in a straight line.

I put my arm around her, pulling her closer as she rested her hand on my leg.

Usually, that wouldn't get too much of a reaction from me. But, seeing that she was sexy and was probably sitting on a fat bank account, her touch got a rise out of me that made her take notice of the print that was bulging through my slacks.

"What's that?"

Her question didn't stop her hand from reaching to investigate. And it damn sure didn't stop her from going for my zipper to do a more thorough investigation, either.

"You really are packing something." She made sure no one was watching, as my zipper made the sound that all men love. Her hand went down into my boxers like she was searching for a buried treasure. I was always stiffer than a white boy trying to dance, and that made it easier for her to grab it and start a two-step of her own.

"So, this is why you're so confident."

Women were always surprised by what God blessed me with, and she wasn't any different. She was stroking it as she snuggled in and put her head on my chest. The scene was set for a blow job by the river on a beautiful night, so I raised up and let her get a palmful of my balls so that they could get in on the action.

"Got me using two hands for this thing."

She smiled up at me and took a kiss while stroking my dick with one hand and massaging my balls with a soft and gentle touch with the other. It was a slow and long kiss, which caused my dick to throb in her grip.

Her focus went back to the task at hand after our tongue-tangling, and I tilted my head back and counted the stars while expecting a little mouth-sex. Her hands were continued to work but I felt no lips or tongue.

"Why haven't you cum yet?"

I don't know what type of limp dick niggas she had been around, but she had me all the way fucked up. Laughing, I replied, "Baby, you got great hands, but it takes more than that to make me bust."

Still stroking, she asked, "How good of a lover are you?"

"How good of lover do you want me to be?"

A slight pause. "Good enough to make me cum."

"Shidddddddd, is that all?" I chuckled and got a soft head-butt to my chest. "You sure don't ask for a lot."

At that moment, she sat up and left my dick swaying like a skyscraper on a windy day.

"I'm not talking about with that," she said, gesturing to my still-swaying skyscraper. "I'm talking about with this."

Her hand came up to my mouth, and she used a French-manicured finger to slowly trace my lips. When it came to a stop, I then returned the favor by sucking and then wrapping my tongue around her finger just to give her a sample of what I had in store for her. From the way she was breathing heavy, I knew she enjoyed it.

"Like I said," replying as she caught her breath. "You sure don't ask for much."

She sucked her teeth, smiling. "I've always been attracted to your confidence."

I watched her get up, look around and straighten out her skirt. Out of nowhere, her entire demeanor changed, and she started speaking in a real business-like manner, her posture upright like a teacher in front of class. She most definitely had my attention.

"A man hasn't made me cum from oral since my first husband, and that's been over twenty years ago. He had a tongue on him, but he was using it any and everybody. I can tell you're the same way."

Shit, I wanted to stop her right there, but she was right, so I let her go on.

"But I don't care about that," she pointed out while staring directly at me. "I just want to cum. And if you make me cum with that mouth, I buy you a brand-new car of your choice, not exceeding fifty-thousand dollars. Do you think you can do that, Mr.?"

To be honest, I was kind of in shock. I played it cool, though. With conviction in my voice to make sure that she felt my words, I replied by saying, "Do a bear shit in the woods and wipe his ass with a rabbit?"

She shook her head while trying not to laugh too hard. "Let's go. I'll pay for the room."

Thirty minutes later, we were in a penthouse suite in one an expensive hotel a few blocks away from the riverfront. As soon as we came in, she headed right to the huge bathroom and started the shower. I was glad of that because ain't nothing like sucking on a fresh pussy. She didn't waste time stripping out of her close and switching her ass to the shower. I was right behind her, thinking about what kind of car I wanted.

We got right to it in the walk-in shower that had a bench and room enough for six people. She grabbed me before the door closed and stuck her tongue down my throat, kissing me like she had been starving for a nigga. My dick was slapping her thighs as we kissed, and she reached down and started pulling like she was trying to milk it dry.

She was a great kisser and she knew how to make a brother feel good, but my mind was now on the new Corvette that was about to be released. With that vision in my head, I decided it was time to make it come to fruition, and her too.

I pulled away from her with my hands still on her waist, surprised that she didn't care about getting her hair wet. The water was splashing in between us as I reached for the complementary body wash that was placed in a basket decorated with plastic rose petals. She grabbed a face towel and held it under the water while I covered it with the fresh-scented body wash. I then took the towel and ran it over her shoulders and down her arm and back up over her breast while she stood there letting the water run through her hair. Her entire body was treated to a slow and sensual scrub while I pictured myself riding to Earth, Wind and Fire in my new car.

"You really know how to treat a woman, I see."

I was behind her, letting the towel massage her back and down to her curvy backside. "I like to think so."

"Well, I haven't cum yet." Challenge was in her voice.

I wasn't about doing a lot of talking at that moment. It was time to make her a believer, and she stepped to the right person to make her one.

I let her rinse off while I kissed the back of her neck and let my dick slide in between her ass cheeks just enough to tease her. She was squirming like she was trying to make it go in, but I pulled back and kept doing what I was doing. She then reached back like she was trying to grab it, and that's when I took her by the waist and guided her to the bench. I put my hand in the middle of her back and she bent her over, her hands resting on the bench as she glanced back at me.

"What you back there doing?" she asked, legs spreading wider and ass tooting up in the air.

I smiled. "We didn't have dessert after dinner, so I think I'll have mine now."

I kneeled down on one knee like I was about to propose, my tongue ready to momentarily make her ass my lawfully wedded wife for this special occasion. It was looking like a caramel cake, so I took my hands and spread her ass cheeks as far as I could and came from the bottom up. My tongue was extended to the max because I wanted that damn car bad as hell. It was the most ass I licked in my entire life. The only thing that was missing, was my ass-eating bib.

When the tip of my tongue hit her asshole, she stood up on her toes like a trained ballerina without uttering a single word. The only sounds were the splattering of the water against the marble floor and the smacking and licking like I was one of the Fat Boys at an all-you-can eat buffet.

I let my hands roam up and down her thighs, rubbing and caressing her how a woman loves to be touched, letting her know that I wasn't going to ignore an inch of her body. I kept in mind that she hadn't cum by oral in a long time, so I wanted to stimulate her entire body before I went in to take care of the business. Some mental stimulation was probably needed to get her where I wanted her to be, so I got in her head in between getting in that ass.

I ran my fingertips across her inner thigh. "Do you feel like a woman right now?

Lick.

She panted. "Very much so."

"I knew you would taste this good when I first laid eyes on you."

Tongue kiss.

She stood up on her toes again and shook her ass slowly, making her ass cheeks slap against my face. "I knew you could work your tongue when I first laid eyes on you," she replied, glancing back with a curled lip.

"You're a smart lady." I let my hand glide up her leg until my thumb felt like it dipped into a warm cup of butter. That ass jiggled again when I gave her long lick. "Do you get this often?"

She hit a high note when I let the tip of my tongue tickle hit that Hersey highway.

"No!" Coming back down on her feet. "Never had it done."

My tongue got hard hearing her say that. It was the motivation to the ultimate booty stimulation. I jabbed my tongue in her to let her know that I was making sure that she was getting her money's worth. I was teasing her clit the entire time, and she was exactly where I wanted her to be.

I ate her ass until she almost lost her balance, and had to hold her by the waist to guide her into the bedroom, where she got up on the bed and caught her breath. Knowing what was at stake, I pulled out ever trick in my bag, starting with some serious toe-sucking. It wasn't something I did often, but it ain't a place on a woman's body where I wouldn't put my mouth and make it feel good to her.

"You are something else," she cooed, looking down at me with her big toe in my mouth. A giggle. "You're a freak, I see."

I ran my tongue across her toe-tips. "No, baby. I'm a pleaser."

"Mmmm." She guided her big toe back into my mouth. "A good one, I might add."

After giving her other foot the same treatment, I moved up and made my way to the place that held the key to my Corvette. That's my favorite color. The color I was focused on was pink, though, and I went to work before she knew what happened.

My tongue was like a ballpoint pen, and I used it to sign my name all over that pussy. She damn near pulled my hair out when

I put my signature sucking/licking combination on her clit, and she would've snatched a plug out if I hadn't yelled.

"Oh, I'm sorry." She had a concerned expression on her face when she stared down to me. My hair was still in her grasp, but she loosened her grip. "Don't stop, though."

I replied with more mouth-work and she went back to hair-pulling, but not as hard. My tongue was lashing her clit like a whip taming a tiger, sending her into a shaking frenzy. I had my arms locked around her legs, so she couldn't do anything but take all I had to give. It fucked me up when she let out a scream and started flopping her head around like the little girl from the movie The Exorcist. Next thing I knew, she went completely still. I looked up with my lips still glued to her clit, hoping she didn't have a damn heart-attack before I got my car. It was a relief to see her chest rising up and down as she breathed.

"You okay?" I gently rubbed her stomach, a slight snore escaping her partly-opened mouth. Seconds later, it was followed by a loud snort.

Her eyes opened, and I could tell that she was surprised by the way she just stared at the ceiling and shook her head. "When you want your car?"

I gave her a slow lick. "We'll talk about that later. I'm not finished yet."

She passed out three more times when I was done, making sure that she would never forget me. The impression she left on me was quite impressive, just the same.

Once she had come as many times as she could, she sat up and asked, "So, what is that dick like."

I chuckled while stroking it a few times. "I thought you'd never ask."

We fucked for the whole night away, and in every room in the hotel. I even bent her over and made her put her hands on the floor-to-ceiling windows and hit her doggy-style while looking out over the city. She came more times than I could count, and she confessed that I was the best lover she ever had while she gave me some of the greatest head I'd ever had.

I got my car a few days later, and we continued our affair for a few years after that. Like all of the women I came across, we eventually drifted apart but always remained friends. She's seventy-seven years old now, and every time we see each other, she stills says that I was the best she ever had. It's something that I take total pride in.

Chapter 7

The Good Life

To do something that we love to do and earn a living from it, is what life's all about. It's the American dream. And, during my thirties and forties, I was living it, baby.

Now, I never called myself a "gigolo", or advertised that I was selling sex. I also never asked a woman for a damn dime. It was just that I dated older women who were established and had money to bring them the joy that they didn't find in marriages or relationships. Women are natural givers and nurturers, and if they loved a man--or anyone for that matter--they would do whatever they could to bring that person happiness, comfort. Throw in an endless supply of orgasms, she'll give you her heart, her mind, and some money. I knew this, and my life was good because I applied it and was rewarded handsomely.

Everything I owned at one point, had been bought or financed by a woman, from my wardrobe, to the cars I drove, to the house I lived in. A woman would invite me to the mall with her and I would come out carrying bags stuff with clothes they picked out for me. I didn't mind them dressing me at all. It was their money and I was just thankful for their generosity.

The majority of the "gifts" I received came in cold hard cash, which is always the best gift. It never bothered me when a woman left a stack of money on the nightstand after we got done taking care of business. In fact, it was flattering to know that women thought so much of my sex game that they didn't mind compensating me for it. I was fucking up a storm and women were making it rain on me big-time.

Chapter 8

Pop-pop

Fucking never seemed like a job until I met this one lady who I called "Pop-pop" because she could pop that pussy for twenty-four hours straight if you let her. My sex drive was extremely high, but hers went through the damn roof. She could ride a dick until the sun came, and get hit from the back until that mofo went down, and all at the ripe age of sixty-years old. She looked twenty years younger and had the stamina of a marathon runner, so it was always a challenge I looked forward to whenever we hooked up. I didn't think I would ever meet a woman who could outlast me, but Pop-pop made me a believer.

The first time I went to see her, she answered the door in some high heels and a red teddy. We had talked before and she asked what my favorite color was, and now she was wearing it. I wanted to drop down and suck on her pussy right then and there for being so thoughtful.

Her hand was around my wrist before I could say hello, pulling me through the door and closing it behind us. I was checking out the nicely furnished living room while she gave me a head-to-toe inspection.

"You smell good, look good, and dressed really nice," she said with a matter-of-fact tone. "How long can you fuck, though?"

She caught me off guard, but I quickly recovered. "As long as you need me to."

That caused her to continue to size me up.

She was a short little thing with a toned frame like she worked out on the regular.

Her hair was pinned up with a few loose curls dangling from each side, and she gave off the vibe like she was used to being in charge. When she reached for my dick and rubbed a few times through my slacks, her facial expression told me that she was impressed. It was then followed by a quizzical look.

"Do you kiss?"

Instead of answering, I showed her. We let our tongues wrestle for a minute or so while she got her rubbed on. When she had enough proof of my kissing ability, she stepped back and gave me another look.

"I hope you ate your Wheaties," she said, taking me by the arm and dragging me to the back of the house.

She opened the door to a room that was occupied by a California king-sized bed and no other furniture. There was only a yellow fitted sheet on the bed and several matching pillows that were coordinated to the color of the walls. It gave the room a bright and lively feel that gave me a little boost of energy that I figured I would need.

"You like mirrors, I see."

"Love them."

It was obvious because they were all over the walls and positioned at bed-level.

Every angle was covered. Either she loved herself that much, or she was just a freaky ass woman, which I hoped was the case.

The mirrors had me, though. Everywhere I looked, I saw myself. Shit was getting me hyped up.

"Make yourself comfortable." She gestured toward the bed.

I took that as my sign to strip, so I came out of my clothes as she monitored my every move. She didn't say anything else until I was asshole naked.

"Just crawl up there and lay flat on your back. I'll take it from there."

I quickly realized that she wasn't bullshitting when she said that.

No soon as I was on my back, she was up on the bed and came in with her attack.

I felt one hand grab my dick and the sweet sensation of her tongue sliding across my balls as she jacked me off to complete stiffness. She made sure both got equal treatment, taking one after the other in her mouth and sucking them like they were giving her life. I sat up on my elbows to get a better view.

"You have some big balls," she said in between licks, running her tongues up the base of my rod. "Some big pretty balls connected to an even prettier dick."

The wrist action she had was that of a professional dick handler. It was slow and steady, and she didn't miss a stroke while she climbed me like King Kong going up the Empire State Building. Once at the top, she admired the view that apparently made her mouth water. It rolled from her lips and landed on the head of my pulsating dick and was quickly followed by the prettiest lips I had seen in years.

She adjusted herself sideways so that she could watch while she sucked on the head until she decided to see how low she could go. I had never run into a woman who could take all of me in, so I wasn't surprised when she stopped about a third of the way down. She came back up and handled what she could, and I smiled sat her for the attempt.

The mirrors seemed to really turn her on, because she started moaning more and more as she stared at her reflection. It was like she was in competition with the woman in the mirror, and she was winning like a mofo. My balls were happy and my dick was rock-solid hard. That's when she raised up and turned to me. That stroke was still going as she got ready to ride the bull.

"Now let's see what you got," she said, cracking a smile as she got on her feet.

The muscles in her nicely toned legs bulged slightly when she squatted over me while she held my dick steady. I could feel the heat when her lips kissed the head and slowly covered came down on it. The strength in her legs was obvious, because she held herself up while rubbing the tip of my dick across her pussy. The whole time, she was looking in the picture-mirror on the wall at the head of the bed.

"Damn, that dick looks good," she whispered in between gasp, the sound of her wetness becoming louder as she teased herself. "Okay, that's it. Give me your hands."

I did as she ordered. Our palms touched and we interlocked fingers. She was sitting like she was in an invisible chair, her gaze in the mirror as my dick started to disappear inside of her. And even though I could feel how tight she was, she didn't seem to be in any pain as she lowered herself until my balls were the only thing left. All she did was exhale like she was practicing her breathing.

"I was wondering if I could take it all," she spoke softly, my dick probably in her chest as she sat still for a brief second. A wiggle in her hips let me know that she was getting a real feel of what she was in for.

"Yeah, you got it," I whispered, encouragement in my voice while she took ever inch I had to offer.

"It's so...so...damn big!"

At that moment, she proceeded to raise her hips and hit me with some pussy control that I had never experienced. It felt like she had my dick in a closed fist as she came up on it, and I could literally feel her grip pulsate the whole time. I caught her looking at me while I was trying to understand what the fuck was going on. A sly grin on her face let me know that she knew exactly what the fuck she was doing, and I honestly, loved that shit. Man, when I say she had that real gripper-type pussy, the kind that men search high and low for, I mean that from the bottom of my heart.

Usually, I'm the one who's putting in work while pleasing the lady I'm with. Not when it came to Pop-pop. She was a world class dick-rider who probably could've won gold medals if dick-riding was an Olympic sport. I was able to do my thing but she seemed to like to be in control the majority of the time. Some women need that control in order orgasm, and I found out that was the case with Pop-pop. Riding was the only way she would come, so I let her play cowgirl as much as she liked.

That gripper thing had my mind blown and dick mesmerized after she put it on me for a couple of minutes. It came to an abrupt halt, though, causing my eyes to open to see my dick swaying side to side. At the foot of the bed was where she was standing, an amused smile on her face.

"Let's start here."

Being in the profession I was in, taking orders from women became commonplace. They paid the cost to be the boss, so I was always an obedient mofo when money was on the line. Whatever they wanted, they got it with a smile.

I raised an eyebrow as I climbed out the bed. "Oh, now we're starting?"

"Yes, and I hope you can reach the finish line."

With those words, she placed her hands on the bed with a deep arch in her back, like a cat stretching before it's ready to play. She then gave the mirror her gaze while I came behind her and began to feel her up.

"Can you take this off?" My hand was already reaching for the strap on her teddy. "I want to see all of your sexy ass."

She stood up and backed into me, my dick stiff against her ass. I started kissing her neck and down her back while sliding the teddy off until it fell to the floor.

"You got what you wanted," she stated, returning her hands to the bed, followed by the arch in her back and ass in the air. "Now give me what I want." She was staring at me through the mirrored wall to our right. When she cocked her leg up on the bed, I knew what she wanted and how she wanted it.

I played along with her by grabbing my dick and aiming it right for the hole. The mirror gave us a beautiful view, and her eyes seemed to get wider as my head hit the hole and started a slow entrance. I put my arm under her leg and lifted it up higher for us to get an even better view.

"Oh, baby, look at that dick go in there." She had an intense look on her face.

"Go deep, baby."

My hips gave her the thrust she was looking for, as I disappeared in her and admired my work. "That's a pretty picture right there."

A gasp. "Yes, now fuck me."

I quickly got to work, hitting her with some long and deep strokes. Her flexibility made it easy for me to raise her leg all the way up and pin it to my shoulder while I jabbed that pussy with everything I had. After a few strokes, I could see her wetness shining on my rod every time I pulled out.

"You better get this pussy," she demanded, giving me a fierce grin as our skin slapped against each other. "Get it, baby!"

A woman talking that shit always turned me on. It made my dick grow even harder and threw me into second gear. I battle-rammed that pussy with her leg on my shoulder while pulling her to me by her waist until she reached back and put her hand on my stomach. When she did that, I slowed my stoke down and held back on giving her every inch. That was a woman's universal sign that I was giving her too much dick.

"I'm trying to take it." She started a slow twerk while I used my hands to slowly massage her body with half of me in her. "But you're the biggest I've had by far."

I was squeezed her ass like it was some Charmin, checking the scene out in the mirror to the right. Our eyes met and we held the stare. I stood still while she gave my dick a slow and sensual ride, an intensity brewing as we looked into each other's eyes.

Her's softened as she cooed, "You're a sexy ass young man."

Before I could say anything, that gripper caused the words to get stuck in my throat. She came back, and then went forward while putting the squeeze on me.

"Girl, you know you ain't right!" I closed my eyes for a second and took it all in.

"You got some vise-grips in that mofo or something."

Her innocent look didn't make her look innocent. "What I do?"

"Yeah, okay." I chuckled. "You know what you be doing?"

She hit me with a last stroke and then turned around with cat-like reflexes. Before I knew it, she was on her knees holding my dick like a prized possession. It didn't take long for her to start using those magic hands of hers, using both to jack me off while I turned into a spectator.

"You got the perfect dick for me." It came as a whisper right before she licked her way up to the top. "Tastes so good too."

I chuckled. "Bon appetit."

Tongue first, she took me in her mouth and, again, enjoyed the mirror show, stopping briefly like she was posing for a picture with my dick damn near hitting her tonsils. That was followed by a one-handed stroke that was timed perfectly with the bobbing of her neck, something that separated the best head-hunters for the rest of the pack. She was looking like a rooster the way she was working it, but I was the one ready to cockle-doodle-doo when she held my dick like a billy club and slapped it against her hanging tongue.

Pat! Pat! Pat! Pat! Pat!

"Ohhhh-weee!"

My reaction caused her to crack a smile and do it again, confidence all in her pose.

Pat! Pat! Pat! Pat! Pat!

"It's so hard!"

Another "Pat! Pat! Pat! Pat! Pat!" before she rose to her feet and got back onto the bed.

"What are you waiting for?" she asked, rolling over on her back.

As I got in the bed, she began to do some leg exercises, lifting, spreading and back together before making like a gymnast and throwing them all the way back until they were touching the pillow her head was propped up on. Bent up like a pretzel with her arms locked around her legs, she looked like she was prepared to take ever inch. I made it to her on my knees and let the tip of my dick rub against her asshole. She was using two fingers to massage her clit.

"I need all of that." She was staring up at me like she wanted to make sure that her message was clear.

"Say no more."

A little motion in my hips landed my dick right on the target. She gave me a sly grin as I entered head-first, my hands resting on the thighs of her pinned-back legs. I was anticipating the gripper to come into play, and she didn't disappoint as I went halfway in.

It was like she had a built-in dick massager. My knees got weak from the heat and the squeeze she was putting on, so I fell forward and was ready to grind in the pussy while I regained my composure. She wasn't haven't it, though. Her two hands went up and caught me before I came down on her.

"I need to see." A bench-press motion was how she got me off her, sending me back on my knees, dick still in her. Her focus was on the ceiling. That's when I realized there was a mirror up there, too.

"Mirror, mirror on the mothafuckin' wall." I laughed and got comfortable on my knees, starting a stroke that she met with some hip movement of her own.

Pretty soon, I was just standing there supplying the dick. She was on her back, looking like she was belly-dancing, hips rolling like a mofo. I was watching the juices build up right before my eyes while her juicy pussy swallowed more and more of me.

"Rub my clit, please."

I licked my thumb and planted it right where she asked, hitting it with a circular motion. "It's my pleasure."

Her squirming sped up when I touched that button, and after flicking the clit a few times, she said those words that I love to hear.

"I'm about to cum."

The motion in her hips picked up and she was working my dick like a washing machine on spin cycle and rinsing it at the same damn time. She was a squirter, and the evidence was streaming up out of her and all over me. I kept my thumb on her clit and watched her wet my stomach up with her juices until she was had squirted her last drop. My dick was soaked and still in her when she came to a stop. She wasn't sweating or breathing like she had just put in some major work, but I knew all the hip-rolling she had done wasn't easy. Shit, I was breathing harder than her and I wasn't doing anything but working my thumb.

"That looks nice."

It was one of the few times when she wasn't in the mirror. Smiling at me with her legs still pinned back, she scooted away enough for my dick to slide out of her. She then reached for it and did the honors of sliding it back in for me. I didn't expect her to hold her hand up to my mouth for me to suck the wetness from her fingers, but I gladly licked every last one of them.

That brought another smile to her face. "Now you can get it how you want, but I do want to see."

"So, you want to see this dick in that pussy, huh?"

Giggle. "Yes. Deep, too."

"Whatever you want while I'm with you." I stared her in the eyes while assuming the pushup position, my throbbing rod enjoying the warmth.

"Well, give it to me, young man."

She put her hands on her thighs like she wanted to open her pussy as wide as she could while I gave her what she wanted. The slow hoola-hoop stroke that I had perfected over time, was what I hit her with first; all hip action and giving her about half of the dick. I always wanted to make sure that I touched every spot, so I made like Clarence Carter and stroked it to the east, stroked it to the west, and once I went all the way in, shit, she had dick all up in her chest. And, obviously, she loved it.

"You're about to get wet."

I could feel the squeeze coming on, so I started pounding that pussy as she began to erupt. "Yeah, baby, make it rain on me."

She grabbed her ankles and started humming loud as hell like a teapot ready to boil over. That's when I felt her sweet hot tea overflow and splatter against my stomach.

I was tempted to quench my thirst and get a taste, but I didn't want to take the chance of interfering with her groove. She was throwing that pussy upward with every thrust in her hips, and I met her halfway. I could feel my balls slap against her ass when our body crashed like a pair of symbols, her juices splashing on contact.

I didn't stop until I felt her release me from that grip of hers. Then her legs sprung forward and landed on my shoulders. I was still snuggled deep inside of her, the wetness turning cold on the sheets below us.

"I didn't get you too wet, did I?" She moved some hair from her eyes and didn't seem to mind that she had sweated out what appeared to be a recently done hairdo.

I chuckled. "Shit, I'm trying to get soaked."

"Say no more," she replied with a sly grin.

Her legs came off my shoulder, and pretty manicured feet planted themselves on my chest. But, before I could reach to suck on a big toe, the wind was damn near knocked out of me when she launched me backwards like a bag of potatoes. The bed was big enough to where I landed at the foot, flat on my back, dick still hard and pointing to the ceiling. All I could hear was her laughing as she jumped on it and started riding me like she was in a fucking rodeo. I just put my hands behind my head and observed my little cowgirl.

Pop-pop rode my dick in every position known to man. If dick-riding was an Olympic sport, she would've easily claimed the gold medal. Her technique was superb and the form she held while rising off my dick was absolutely of elite caliber. And I really didn't do much but lay there except for the occasion thrust. She obviously loved to be in control, and from the way she was squirting every five minutes, it had to be her preferred position.

After an hour of her throwing that pussy on me with all her might, and me looking like I had just gotten out the shower from the neck down, she lifted up and grabbed hold of my rod.

"You don't mind, do you?"

I didn't know what she was talking about until I raised my head to see her on both feet aiming my dick straight for her asshole. "I don't mind at all," I replied with a chuckle. "Just don't hurt yourself."

"You worry about yourself." She gasped as she lowered herself down onto me. "I can handle whatever you got."

The tightness was too much for me to just lay there, and I was wanted to see if she could really back up that talk. So, as she eased on down further, I grabbed her ankles and helped myself deeper inside of her.

"Oh, shit!"

I started coaching her. "You're fine. You can handle it."

I was telling her that she could handle it, but I was the one who could bust a nut at that very moment. Her ass was had that gripper too. And, when she got herself adjusted and was seated comfortably on it all the way, it didn't take long for her to buckle down and start her fantastic voyage. A few strokes in and I had to let my mind wonder to sports just so I wouldn't cum. Pop-pop turned out to be the only woman who could fuck me under the table. We fooled around for years after that first meet, but I never gave her the satisfaction of knowing that.

A sight that would probably live with me forever is watching Pop-pop play with her pussy while she had every inch of my dick up her ass. She was on her feet, one hand used for balance while she furiously rubbed her clit with the other. It was done so effortlessly like anything else she did, and the results were the same.

"I'm about to squirt again."

She took two fingers and jammed them in her pussy, fucking herself briefly before she parted the lips with two fingers and squirted a stream that sprayed me like a fire extinguisher. I opened my mouth but came up short when it splattered all over my stomach and chest.

Pop-pop noticed my effort and decided to help me out a bit by hopping off and climbing up my chest until her pussy was hovering over my face. A bend in her knees and I had a mouth full of her sweetness, tongue extended, at the ready. I was waiting for her to come all the way down and smother me with the pussy, but those strong ass legs of hers allowed her to still remain in control while she fed me at her pleasure.

"Just keep your tongue like that," she cooed, her hips swaying back and forth. It was touching every desired spot, and when she added some finger action to her clit, a warning came right after. "I'm about to squirt, baby."

"That was the plan, right?" I chuckled, extending my tongue as far as I could.

The first blast reminded me of getting shot in the eye with a water gun when I was a kid. It caught my ass off guard, but I blinked it off and waited for the next shot, mouth open at the ready while she rubbed and unleashed a quiet storm. Sprinkles of her juices splattered on my tongue and trickled down my chin and onto my chest. She was breathing heavily as she rubbed until she hit empty. I was then inclined to take matters into my own mouth.

Lifting my head up, I gave her pussy a passionate tongue kiss, trying my best fill her up with my mouth. Those strong legs of hers buckled when I took a long suck on her clit, so I knew I was handling my business. She then took it upon herself and fell to the bed, my tongue following her lead and landing right on that pussy when her ass touched the mattress.

I dove in and left my name cemented in the memory of her uterus, not stopping until she begged me to after a couple of hours of fine dining on her clit.

She I thought she would've been down for the count, but it seemed like she had time to recover and regain some energy. When she gave me that devilish grin after catching her breath, I just rode over and got in position.

My dick needed to be put in a sling when Pop-pop shot her last rain shower down on me as the clock hit six a.m. That made ten hours of continuous fucking and I don't know how it was done.

Getting some sleep was definitely on my mind when she climbed out the bed and came back minutes later with a warm and soapy towel. She washed me up really good as

I laid there, and even kissed the head of my dick when she was done.

I must've nodded off for a second, because when I opened my eyes, Pop-pop was standing over me wearing a housecoat. She also had a stack of money in her hand.

"Thanks for a good time." She had a pleasant smile on your face. "I will call you when I need you."

I wasn't the sharpest knife in the drawer, but from what I was seeing and hearingshe was playing me like a two-dollar whore. It was a few hundred-dollar bills on top of the stack she was holding, so I knew I was worth more than two bucks. I guess I was used to fucking and sucking a woman to sleep, and eventually falling asleep next to her.

It was the first time that I felt used, like a piece of toilet paper after whipping somebody's ass. I shook the feeling off as I sat up and got out of her bed.

The money was still in her extended hand. She didn't say another word after I took it and put my clothes on. We fucked for years after that, but I never went to her house again.

Closing remarks

Now, I will save the rest of the stories of the numerous women I've made love to during my life for a later date. My dick still gets hard without Viagra, and my tongue game only gets better with time, so I know I have a few more chapters in me. But one thing I want you to understand is that when I say, "made love to", it has nothing to do with having feelings for someone while having sex. It's simply about pleasing that person to the point that they love everything you do at that given moment while sex is taking place. It's about loving their body and doing whatever it takes for them to fully enjoy sharing their body with you. So, yes, you don't have to love someone to make love to them. That's all I'm saying.

When making love to a woman, she loves to be held kissed and caressed. A woman never wants to be rushed while making love (I didn't say "having sex"). Before the actual lovemaking starts, hit her with a little foreplay to discover those spots that really get her going. That gets them relaxed and puts them in more of a sexy mood. Try kissing her on the lips and then trace her lip line with the tip of your tongue. A lot of women love. Two kissers with chemistry will have her pussy wet and makes for a hard dick.

Use that tongue more. Make sure you explore every part of her body. Put some effort into making her pussy wet and purr for your touch. It's no place on a woman's body that my tongue hasn't been, and it has worked wonders for me. The tongue is the sword that men can yield mightily if used correctly and get the desired results that he's looking for. At least for me.

Don't be in a rush to stick the dick in. The pussy isn't going anywhere, and it's like pizza: it's always better when it's hot. Try some sex toys to really get her in the mood to satisfy you to the fullest. A lot of women love sex toys. I knew one woman who loved when I had a dick in her ass and a dildo in her pussy. Different strokes for different folks, and our job as men, is to find what stroke fits that person. That's our only job in the bedroom, fellas.

So, like I said, I'll be back with a few more stories to tell. In the meantime, please her like she deserves to be pleased. If not, send her my way and I'll show her how I treat my lady.